Who Are You?

Celtic Tree Astrology

Virginia Loh-Hagan

45TH PARALLEL PRESS

Published in the United States of America by Cherry Lake Publishing Group
Ann Arbor, Michigan
www.cherrylakepublishing.com

Reading Adviser: Marla Conn, MS, Ed., Literacy specialist, Read-Ability, Inc.
Book Designer: Felicia Macheske

Photo Credits: © NinaMalyna/Shutterstock.com, cover; © Helga Chirk/Shutterstock.com, cover; © Christopher Elwell/Shutterstock.com, cover; © Denis Belitsky/Shutterstock.com, 5; © Tntk/Shutterstock.com, 6; © Sari ONeal/Shutterstock.com, 9; © Attila JANDI/Shutterstock.com, 11; © tomertu/Shutterstock.com, 12; © Martin Novak/Shutterstock.com, 15; © Dmitry Naumov/Shutterstock.com, 17; © ymgerman/Shutterstock.com, 18; © solarseven/Shutterstock.com, 22; © Master1305/Shutterstock.com, 25; © mark reinstein/Shutterstock.com, 27; © alexkich/Shutterstock.com, 29; © Eric Isselee/Shutterstock.com, 31

Graphics Throughout: © AKaiser/Shutterstock.com; © galastudio/Shutterstock.com; © tanyabosyk/Shutterstock.com; © ViSnezh/Shutterstock.com; © MARINA ARABADZHI/Shutterstock.com; © Alisa Burkovska/Shutterstock.com

45th Parallel Press is an imprint of Cherry Lake Publishing Group.

Library of Congress Cataloging-in-Publication Data

Names: Loh-Hagan, Virginia, author.
Title: Celtic tree astrology / by Virginia Loh-Hagan.
Description: Ann Arbor, Michigan : Cherry Lake Publishing, 2020.
| Series: Who are you? | Includes index.
Identifiers: LCCN 2020006899 (print) | LCCN 2020006900 (ebook)
| ISBN 9781534169203 (hardcover) | ISBN 9781534170889 (paperback)
| ISBN 9781534172722 (pdf) | ISBN 9781534174566 (ebook)
Subjects: LCSH: Astrology, Celtic—Juvenile literature. | Calendar, Celtic—Juvenile literature. | Trees—Miscellanea—Juvenile literature.
Classification: LCC BF1714.C44 L64 2020 (print) | LCC BF1714.C44 (ebook) | DDC 133.5/93916—dc23
LC record available at https://lccn.loc.gov/2020006899
LC ebook record available at https://lccn.loc.gov/2020006900

Cherry Lake Publishing Group would like to acknowledge the work of the Partnership for 21st Century Learning, a Network of Battelle for Kids. Please visit *http://www.battelleforkids.org/networks/p21* for more information.

Printed in the United States of America
Corporate Graphics

Dr. Virginia Loh-Hagan is an author, university professor, and former classroom teacher. She was born on June 14. This makes her an Oak. She lives in San Diego, California, with her very tall husband and very naughty dogs. To learn more about her, visit www.virginialoh.com.

Chapter One

Sacred Trees

Who are the Celts and Druids?

What is Celtic tree astrology?

The **Celts** were **ancient** people from Great Britain and Ireland. Ancient means from a long time ago. **Druids** were Celtic priests. They were educated. They served as teachers and judges. They performed **rites** in forests. Rites are religious events.

Celts thought trees were sacred. They thought people were connected to trees. To them, trees held important wisdom. They believed the world existed in the form of a tree. Tree roots grow deep below the ground. To the Celts, this represented the past. Tree trunks are on land. They're part of everyday life. This represented the present. Tree branches reach up into the sky. They represented the future and the **afterlife**. Afterlife refers to what happens after death.

Read about Yggdrasil, the Norse World Tree.
How is the Norse idea connected to the Celtic idea?

The Celts believed trees represented balance, long life, and strength. They also believed trees represented **rebirth**. Rebirth is being born again. Trees shed leaves in the fall. They grow new leaves in the spring.

Celts had their own **astrology** system. Astrology is a practice. It looks at how natural objects, like trees, affect human lives. Druids served as astrologers. They based their astrology on trees. They **divined** information about people's lives. To divine means to interpret. Druids connected people's personalities to seasons they were in.

Celtic tree astrology is based on people's birth dates. Birth dates are important. The Celts believed they formed people's personalities. They guided people's actions.

Druids noticed patterns in people's lives.
What are some patterns in your life?

FUN FACTS

* There's also Celtic animal astrology. Each animal has its own personality type. Some astrologists merge the Celtic tree and animal profiles. This gives a fuller picture of a person's personality. The connection between animals and people was deep. Some Celts believed they became their animals upon death.

* Giant sequoia trees are among the world's tallest trees. They have the thickest bark. They have tannin. This keeps them from getting sick. The oldest living sequoia is called the "President." It's over 3,200 years old. The largest sequoia is called General Sherman. Its trunk weighs as much as 15 blue whales.

* There are myths about Druids climbing oak trees. Druids did this to get mistletoe. Mistletoe was thought to make living things fertile. It was thought to fight against poisons. Pliny the Elder was an ancient Roman. He said Druids used mistletoe in rites. He said they did this on the fifth day of the moon.

Celtic tree astrology is based on moon cycles. This means the Celtic tree calendar has 13 months. Each month has 28 days. There's 1 extra day. That day is December 23. It's called Nameless Day. It has powers of change.

There are 13 tree signs. Each moon phase has a tree sign. Each tree has its own powers. These powers are connected to people's personalities.

Tree signs are divided into a new moon and a full moon. The first 2 weeks are the new moon. People born during this time are **introverted**. Introverted means shy. The last 2 weeks are the full moon. People born during this time are **extroverted**. Extroverted means outgoing.

Anything is possible on December 23. What would you do on that day?

Chapter Two

Tree Roots

What is Ogham? Who is Robert Graves?

Each Celtic tree sign is connected to a guardian animal. It's connected to a Celtic god. It's connected to gemstones. Most importantly, it's connected to an **Ogham** letter. Ogham is an ancient alphabet. It looks like lines and slashes. Some say it looks like stems and twigs.

Most of the letters are names of trees. Celts believed a tree's magical powers come from the Ogham.

Ogham dates back to the 4th century. Ancient Celts wrote the Ogham letters on wood. They also wrote on stone. The alphabet is named after Ogmios. He's the Celtic god of poetry. (Sometimes, he's called Ogam or Ogma.)

About 400 Ogham tablets have been discovered. Why is it important to protect these tablets?

Historians study history. They think Ogham was used for different reasons. Ogham was used to record people and places. It was used as records for property.

Some historians thought Ogham was used as a secret language. Celts used Ogham to talk to each other. They used it so their enemies couldn't understand them. Ogham may have been the Druids' secret language.

Druids shared their knowledge **orally**. Orally means by speech. They didn't write much down. They didn't want others to learn about their ways. They didn't want their secrets to be in the wrong hands.

Celts believed fairies lived in certain trees. This may be a reason why trees are special. Do you believe in fairies?

EXPLAINED BY
SCIENCE

Trees have a woody stem. They're perennial. Perennial means they can live for many years. Tree leaves take in sunlight. Sun is needed to grow. Trees have bark. Bark is like the tree's skin. It protects trees from animals. It protects trees from sickness. Bark helps trees grow. Most trees grow over 13 feet (4 meters) tall. New cells grow on the tips of branches. This is how trees grow taller. Trees have roots in the ground. These roots collect water and nutrients from soil. They grow at the tip like branches. This is how trees grow deeper. Trees grow wider in their trunks and branches. This growth takes place at the outer layer. This outer layer is called cambium. Cambium stops growing during cold months. This causes tree trunks to develop rings. Each ring represents a year of growth. Counting tree rings tells us how old trees are.

Robert Graves was a poet. He made Celtic tree astrology popular for the modern age. He wrote a book in 1948 called *The White Goddess*. It mentioned a tree goddess. This goddess was like Mother Earth. She was the Queen of the Druids. She ruled over birth, love, and death. She protected trees. She protected knowledge. She was connected to the moon's phases. Her name means oak trees.

Graves said Ogham letters were part of a special calendar. This calendar was the key to ancient rites. This led to ideas about a "tree calendar." Historians criticized Graves. They said his ideas weren't based on Celtic beliefs.

Druids divined future events by listening to leaves rustle in the wind. What do you hear when leaves rustle?

Chapter Three

Branches of Life

What are the 13 Celtic tree types?

The birch tree is the **primary** tree. Primary means main. Birch types are achievers. They have a lot of goals. They're leaders. They work hard. They make their dreams come true. They try new things. They're tough. But they can have quick tempers. Their Ogham letter is B for Beith.

Rowan tree types are thinkers. They have sharp minds. They're creative. They have big ideas. They're full of energy. They're good at getting people to do things. But they can be distant. They can feel misunderstood. Their Ogham letter is L for Luis.

Ash types are free spirits. They're charming. They have big imaginations. They're artists. They sense things. They're good at reading people. But they can be easily distracted and unreliable. Their Ogham letter is N for Nuin.

Birch types are born during the darkest time of the year. They seek out light. Do you know anyone born under the Birch sign?

Alder types are **trailblazers**. Trailblazers are the first to do things. These types motivate others. They have a way with words. They mingle easily. They love being around people. They're confident. They're focused. They don't waste time. But they can be impatient. Their Ogham letter is F for Fearn.

Willow types are watchers. They notice everything. They're really smart. They like learning. They want to know as much as they can. They're patient. They're sensitive. They see the positive in things. But sometimes they can be stubborn. Their Ogham letter is S for Saille.

Hawthorn types are the entertainers. They have different sides. They're playful. They're not all they appear to be. They're curious. They're mysterious. They easily adapt to things. But they can be hard to predict. Their Ogham letter is H for Huath.

Trees are all around you.
What is your favorite tree?

Oak types are the strongest. They're teachers. They have special gifts. They protect the weak. They speak for those without a voice. They're generous. They're kind. They're helpful. But they can be too controlling. Their Ogham letter is D for Duir.

Holly types are rulers. They're noble. They rise to the top. They handle challenges well. They like to win. They're quick learners. They like things to be perfect. But they can be too fussy. They can get bored. They can be lazy. Their Ogham letter is T for Tinne.

Hazel types know things. They're great students. They remember things. They're planners. They're organized. But they can have a hard time making decisions. They can be late. Their Ogham letter is C for Coll.

Oak types are the most stable signs.
Why is it important to be stable?

REAL-LIFE
CONNECTION

Tree sitting is a form of protest. People sit in trees. Sometimes, they sit in tree houses. They do this to stop others from cutting down trees. They want to save forests. A tree village has several tree houses. There was a tree village in Northern California. It was called the Fern Gully Tree-Sit. People did this to protect the giant redwood trees. It lasted 20 years. It ended in 2008. This is when the last 2 people climbed down. They climbed down when promised the trees wouldn't be cut down. Nadia Berg was one of the last 2 climbers. She calls herself Cedar. She lived 200 feet (61 m) off the ground. She did this for 11 months. She called her tree house Grandma. She was 22 years old. She said, "I feel so honored that I could be here for the trees."

Vine types are life lovers. They like good food. They like to have fun. They see both good and bad. But they may have a hard time picking sides. They may change their minds a lot. Their Ogham letter is M for Muin.

Ivy types are survivors. They overcome troubles. They're loyal. They're caring. They're helpful. They forgive easily. They care more about others than themselves. But they can be unsure of themselves. Their Ogham letter is G for Gort.

Reed types are truth-seekers. They dig deep to find meaning. They're good listeners. They keep secrets. They have a strong sense of honor. But they can be **manipulative**. Manipulative means tricking people. Their Ogham letter is Ng for Ngetal.

Elder types are seekers. They love freedom. They're wild. They live life in the moment. They love adventures. They're thoughtful. But they can be reckless. Their Ogham letter is R for Ruis.

Trees are used for many things. Examples are heat, cooking, building materials, and weapons. How do you use trees?

Chapter Four

Famous Examples

Who is Wolfgang Amadeus Mozart? Who is Ruth Bader Ginsburg? Who is Maya Angelou?

Wolfgang Amadeus Mozart was born on January 27, 1756. This makes him a Rowan. Mozart was very creative. He had a lot of energy. He was a famous **composer**. Composers are people who write music. Mozart was a child **prodigy**. A prodigy is a child with amazing skills or talents. Mozart played piano and violin at an early age. He started composing at 5 years old. He performed in front of kings and queens. He traveled all over Europe. He composed over 600 songs. He helped develop **classical** music. Classical music includes symphonies, concertos, operas, and sonatas. These are special musical forms. Mozart's work inspired many people. His music is played all the time.

Who are your favorite musicians?
Look up their Celtic tree signs.

Ruth Bader Ginsburg was born on March 15, 1933. This makes her an Ash. She understands people very well. In fact, she judges them! She's a **justice** on the U.S. Supreme Court. Justices are judges. The Supreme Court is the highest court in the land. Ginsburg is the second woman to be appointed to the Supreme Court.

She's a powerful force. She's her own person. She fights for women's rights. She fights for the rights of workers. She inspires many. She said, "I . . . try to teach through my opinions, through my speeches, how wrong it is to judge people on the basis of what they look like, color of their skin, whether they're men or women."

Read about all the tree types.
What other types would be good judges?

SPOTLIGHT

BIOGRAPHY

Rachel Malarich lives in Los Angeles, California. She's the city's first forest officer. She's in charge of the city's urban forest. Urban means having to do with cities. Her goal is to plant 90,000 trees by the end of 2021. She also wants to increase shade in low-income areas. This is part of the city's Green New Deal. This plan is to make the city of Los Angeles the largest urban forest in the United States. The city mayor said, "Rachel has the vision, experience, and expertise necessary to lead the work . . . building a greener tomorrow." Malarich was a 6th-grade math and science teacher in the early 2000s. She has over 12 years of experience working with trees. She's an arborist. Arborists are people trained to take care of trees. Her favorite trees are the coast live oaks. She said, "They support over 300 species of birds and insects. They're just beautiful."

Maya Angelou was born on April 4, 1928. This makes her an Alder. She was definitely a trailblazer. She fought for the rights of African Americans. She said, "If you don't like something, change it. If you can't change it, change your attitude."

She was an African American poet. She was a civil rights activist. She wrote many important books. She wrote about her life. She lived in a time when African Americans were treated unfairly. She used her pain to help others. She paved a path for others. She was awarded the Presidential Medal of Freedom. She had many words of wisdom. Her words are quoted often.

Look up quotes from Maya Angelou. Which one is your favorite?

WHO ARE YOU?

TAKE THE QUIZ!

Which tree type are you? People are connected to trees. They share similar traits.

- **December 24–January 20:** Birch
- **January 21–February 17:** Rowan
- **February 18–March 17:** Ash
- **March 18–April 14:** Alder
- **April 15–May 12:** Willow
- **May 13–June 9:** Hawthorn
- **June 10–July 7:** Oak
- **July 8–August 4:** Holly
- **August 5–September 1:** Hazel
- **September 2–September 29:** Vine
- **September 30–October 27:** Ivy
- **October 28–November 24:** Reed
- **November 25–December 23:** Elder

Which tree types are you most compatible with? There are certain tree types that match you better than others.

- **Birch:** Willow, Vine, and Ivy
- **Rowan:** Hawthorn and Ivy
- **Ash:** Oak, Holly, and Reed
- **Alder:** Hazel and Elder
- **Willow:** Birch, Hazel, and Vine
- **Hawthorn:** Hazel, Vine, and Birch
- **Oak:** Ash and Reed
- **Holly:** Ash and Elder
- **Hazel:** Willow and Alder
- **Vine:** Birch and Willow
- **Ivy:** Birch, Rowan, and Hawthorn
- **Reed:** Ash and Oak
- **Elder:** Alder and Holly

DISCLAIMER: All the quizzes and questions in this book are designed for entertainment purposes only. They shouldn't be used as advice. They shouldn't be taken seriously. There is no guarantee of accuracy. But they're fun! To download a copy of this quiz, please visit: https://cherrylakepublishing.com/teaching_guides.

What is your guardian animal? Each tree type has a special animal that protects that person.

- **Birch:** Stag or Deer
- **Rowan:** Cat
- **Ash:** Snake
- **Alder:** Fox
- **Willow:** Bull or Cow
- **Hawthorn:** Seahorse
- **Oak:** Wren
- **Holly:** Horse
- **Hazel:** Salmon
- **Vine:** Swan
- **Ivy:** Butterfly
- **Reed:** Wolf
- **Elder:** Hawk or Falcon

What are your lucky colors? There are colors connected to tree types.

- **Birch:** White
- **Rowan:** Gray
- **Ash:** Green
- **Alder:** Red
- **Willow:** Light Yellow
- **Hawthorn:** Purple
- **Oak:** Black
- **Holly:** Silver
- **Hazel:** Brown
- **Vine:** Pink (Pastels)
- **Ivy:** Blue
- **Reed:** Orange
- **Elder:** Gold

GLOSSARY

afterlife (AF-tur-life) the life after death

ancient (AYN-shuhnt) from a time long ago

astrology (uh-STRAH-luh-jee) the practice of how space objects like stars affect the lives of humans

Celts (KELTS) ancient people from Great Britain and Ireland

classical (KLAS-ih-kuhl) music that includes symphonies, concertos, operas, and sonatas

composer (kuhm-POH-zur) person who writes music

divined (dih-VINED) discovered or interpreted

Druids (DROO-idz) Celtic priests

extroverted (EK-struh-vurt-id) outgoing, social

historians (his-TOR-ee-uhnz) experts who study and interpret history

introverted (IN-truh-vurt-id) shy, quiet

justice (JUHS-tis) a judge on the U.S. Supreme Court

manipulative (muh-NIP-yuh-luh-tiv) tricking people to get one's way

Ogham (OH-gum) ancient Celtic alphabet that looks like stems and twigs

orally (OR-uhl-ee) by speech

primary (PRYE-mair-ee) main

prodigy (PRAH-dih-jee) a child with amazing skills or talents

rebirth (ree-BURTH) cycle of life and death

rites (RITES) religious ceremonies

trailblazers (TRAYL-blayz-urz) people who start things and pave the way for others

INDEX